...ures and often tells stories, all of it magic and all of it true.

...res and all of the stories, and all of the magic, the music is you.

- John Denver -

I DEDICATE THIS BOOK TO GLENN & MUFFY AND IN LOVING MEMORY O
YOUR GIFTS OF SUNSHINE WARM MY HEART AND SPIRIT EVERYDAY.–

The publishers wish to thank children's literary agent Sandy Ferguson Fuller of Alp Arts Company, Golden, Colorado,
idea (while John Denver was still alive) of bringing John's spirit to children through picture books, and even after his
Hal Thau, John's long-time friend and business manager, who consistently supported the project; Jim Bell of Bell Lice
and Michael Connelly and Keith Hauprich of Cherry Lane Music Publishing Company, who put it together; the Warr
for their support; and BMG Music Company for their courtesy with respect to "The Music Is

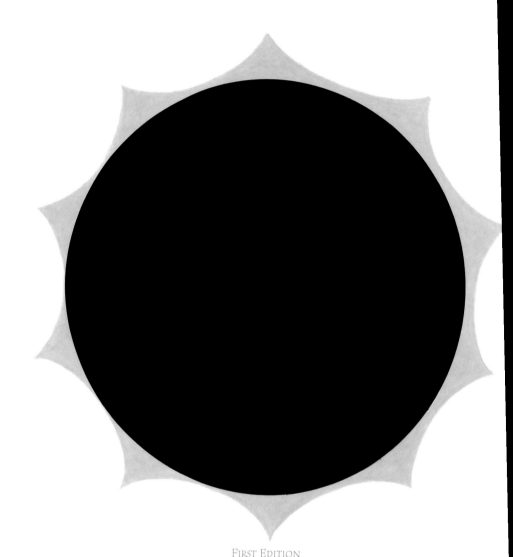

FIRST EDITION
10  9  8  7  6  5  4  3  2  1
A Sharing Nature With Children Book
Book Design by Christopher Canyon   Production by Christopher Canyon & Andrea Miles   Prepress by Andrea Mile
Copyright © 2003 Dawn Publications / Illustrations copyright © 2003 Christopher Canyon

Library of Congress Cataloging-in-Pul

Canyon, Christopher.
    John Denver's Sunshine on my shoulders / adapted & illustrated
    p. cm.
"A Sharing Nature With Children Book."
Summary: A picture book adaptation of John Denver's song S
celebrates the simple things in life such as sunshine, being in na
    ISBN 1-58469-048-8 (hardback with CD) -- ISBN 1-58469-0
    -- ISBN 1-58469-050-X (pbk.)
    1.  Children's songs--Texts. [1. Sunshine--Songs and music. 2.
I. Title: Sunshine on my shoulders. II. Denver, John. III. Title.
    PZ8.3.C1925Jo 2003
    782.42--dc21

John Denver's
# Sunshine On My Shoulders

Adapted & Illustrated by Christopher Canyon

DAWN PUBLICATIONS

Sunshine on my shoulders

makes me happy,

Sunshine in my eyes

can make me cry.

Sunshine on the water

looks so lovely,

Sunshine almost always makes me high.

If I had a day
that I could give you,

I'd give to you a day just like today.

If I had a song
that I could sing for you,
I'd sing a song to make you feel this way.

Sunshine on my shoulders
makes me happy,

Sunshine in my eyes can make me cry.

Sunshine on the water
looks so lovely.

Sunshine almost always makes me high.

If I had a tale that I could tell you,

I'd tell a tale

sure to make you smile.

If I had a wish
that I could wish for you,

I'd make a wish
for sunshine all the while.

Sunshine on my shoulders makes me happy,

Sunshine in my eyes can make me cry.

Sunshine on the water

looks so lovely,

Sunshine almost always makes me high,

Sunshine almost

all the time makes me high,

Sunshine almost always...

John Denver knew that the most wonderful things in life are simple and free. Things like sunshine and friendship. He shared his feelings in poetry and song—and with his remarkably expressive voice, millions of people responded. "People everywhere are the same in heart and spirit," he said. "No matter what language we speak, what color we are, the form of our politics or the expression of our love and our faith, music proves it: we are the same." He wrote "Sunshine On My Shoulders" during the difficult times of the Vietnam War. It was a tonic for anxiety, and a reminder of the good, pure things in life. As John said, "when things were seemingly out of control, here was a dove coming back with news of dry land. Or at least a song that soared upward, and took its audience back home." It hit the top of the charts, along with many of his other songs. Over 32 million John Denver albums have sold in the United States alone, making him one of the top selling vocal artists of all time.

*Photo courtesy of Lowell Norman*

**John Denver's son Zak gets a ride.**

As a child, Christopher Canyon was deeply touched by John Denver. "John's songs gave me hope, joy, and an unbounded belief in possibilities," he says. "'Sunshine On My Shoulders' is a beautiful, moving song of giving, sharing and appreciation. I feel the most powerful aspect of the song is its pure sincerity." Christopher is an award winning artist, musician and performer dedicated to sharing the joy and importance of the arts with children, educators and families. He frequently visits schools, providing entertaining and educational programs and is a popular speaker at conferences throughout the country. "Everyone has what it takes to be artistic, and it's not talent. It is our creativity," he says. "As humans we are all creative beings and our individual creativity is one of our most powerful gifts. If we celebrate and use our creativity it is amazing how much we can learn, how much we can discover and how much joy we have." This is the seventh book Christopher Canyon has illustrated for Dawn Publications. Previous titles include *The Tree in the Ancient Forest; Stickeen: John Muir and the Brave Little Dog; Wonderful Nature, Wonderful You;* and the Earth trilogy, *Earth & Me, Earth & You,* and *Earth & Us.* He lives in historic German Village in Columbus, Ohio with his artist wife Jeanette Canyon and their three feline children.

Yet John Denver was much more than an entertainer. He believed that everyone can make a difference, so he put his feelings into action. He co-founded the Hunger Project, which is committed to ending world hunger forever (www.thp.org). He created Plant-It 2000, now renamed Plant-It 2020, an organization that has already planted one million trees (www.plantit2020.org.). He bought nearly 1000 acres of spectacular Colorado land and gave it to the Windstar Foundation (www.wstar.org) to carry on environmental education. He was a director and supporter of over 22 environmental organizations including the National Wildlife Federation, Save The Children, the Cousteau Society, Friends of the Earth, and the Human/Dolphin Foundation.

Even with all of his charitable activity, he kept writing songs and singing until his death in 1997 when a small experimental plane that he was soloing (John loved to fly!) crashed into the Pacific Ocean. This book and ones to follow, featuring some of his other songs, are dedicated to bringing to children the message of sunshine.

DAWN PUBLICATIONS
A SHARING NATURE WITH CHILDREN BOOK

Dawn Publications is dedicated to inspiring in children a deeper understanding and appreciation for all life on Earth. Some titles present particular animals, habitats or aspects of nature; others focus on more universal qualities. In each case, our purpose is to encourage a life-long bond with the natural world. To review our titles, please visit us at www.dawnpub.com, or call 800-545-7475.